Go Pea !

BY CHRIS SONNENBURG

PICTURES BY JOE MOSHIER
&
CHRIS SONNENBURG

A CONDUCT HAPPINESS STORYBOOK

Dedicated to
Arianna & Catalina
and
Giovanna, Danica, & Diego
You GO! Girls! and Boy!

A Conduct Happiness Story Book

conducthappiness.com
www.facebook.com/gopeago

Edited by Tamara L. Rice

Special thanks to our wonderful co-conductors
Robyn Moshier
&
Janelle Sonnenburg

Mr. Toast © appears courtesy of Dan Goodsell
visit www.theimaginaryworld.com
&
Tofu Robot © appears courtesy of Scott Brown
visit www.spicybrown.com

This is Pea Freely,
you may already know.

But he can't say hello.
He must...

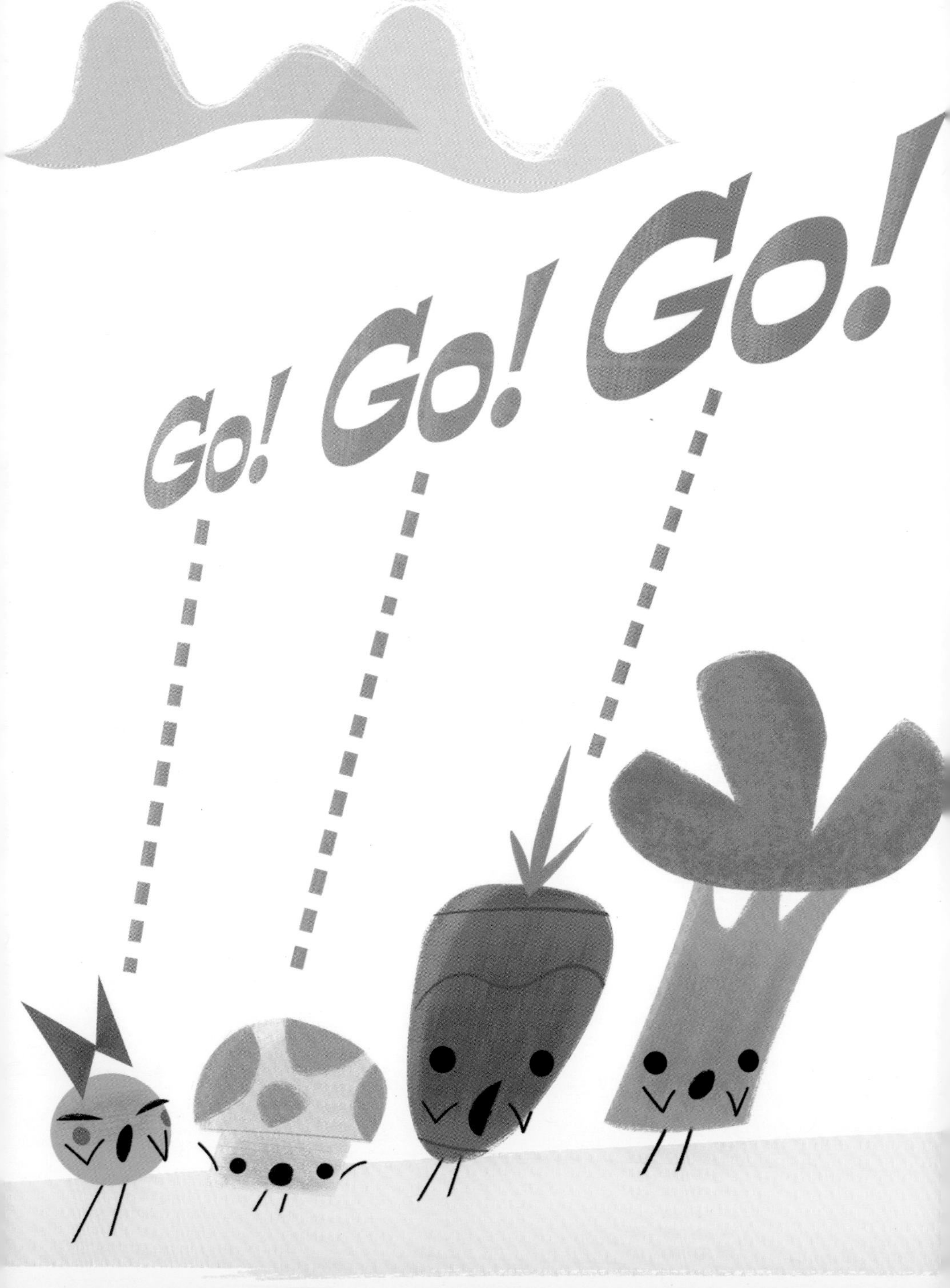
Go! Go! Go!

GO!

"I CAN DO IT," he says.
It's his favorite new phrase.

It SHOUD be, you see,
he's been training for DAYS!

He might want to stop for some old fashioned fun. But he CAN'T at this moment, he must . . .

...RUN, RUN, RUN, RUN, RUN! GO PEA, GO!

He can't stop for a game.

He won't sing in the rain.

He won't take a ride on the town's
new steam train! GO PEA, GO!

He won't stop for a chat.
He won't shop for new hats.

He won't bust a
move with the
"Get Fresh Krew" cats!

He can't stop at the pool!
There's no time for a dip.

He's already the coolest:
"Hey, Pea! Wow, you're hip."
GO PEA , GO!

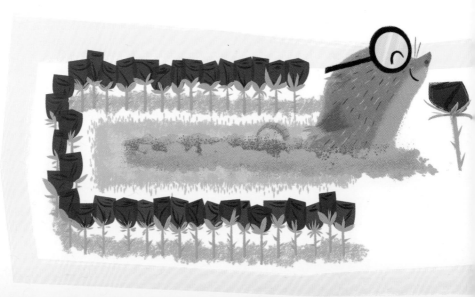

He may WANT to stop shortly and smell all the flowers. But after he wins he'll have plenty of hours.

He can't go for a stroll.
He can't stop for a roll.

For his destination
is that giant
"PEA BOWL."

He wants to just stop and say,
"Hey, man, forget it."
But if he does THAT,
he will REALLY regret it!
GO PEA, GO!

He's tired and lonely
and is losing his spirit.

But he's close to the finish,
so close he can hear it!

He's gettin' too tired!

DO YOU THINK HE CAN MAKE IT?

OUR little Pea has MADE IT!
HEY! What do you think?

NOW he'll take
time to wash his
hands clean in
the sink!

Pea didn't give up.
He wasn't distracted.
So when YOU go to the potty,
act just like PEA acted.

Remember our friend, this cute little green guy.
The steadfast Pea Freely will help you stay dry.

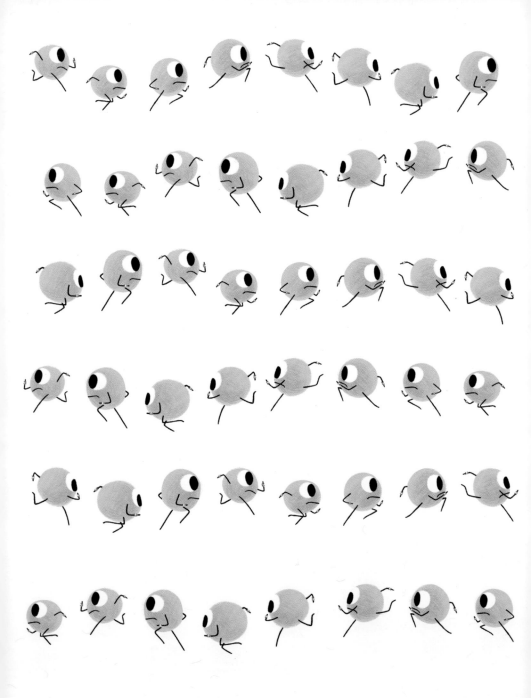

READY, SIT, GO!!
A Pea Freely Potty Chart
Place a sticker on a star each time YOU go!

YOU DID IT!